THE
LOST
DROP

For Flo, for your patience with a slow learner.
G. L.

The Lost Drop
Text copyright © 2023 Grégoire Laforce
Illustration copyright © 2023 Benjamin Flouw
Copyright © Milky Way Picture Books

Editorial and art direction by Nadine Robert
Book design by Jolin Masson
Proofreading by Nick Frost

This edition published in 2023 by Milky Way Picture Books,
an imprint of Comme des géants inc. Varennes, Quebec, Canada.

Library and Archives Canada cataloguing in publication

Title: The lost drop / Grégoire Laforce; illustrations, Benjamin Flouw.
Names: Laforce, Grégoire, author. | Flouw, Benjamin, 1986- illustrator.
Identifiers: Canadiana 20230052673 | ISBN 9781990252297 (hardcover)
Classification: LCC PS8623.A3597 L67 2023 | DDC jC843/.6—dc23

ISBN: 978-1-990252-29-7

Printed and bound in China

Milky Way Picture Books
38 Sainte-Anne Street
Varennes, QC J3X 1R5
Canada

www.milkywaypicturebooks.com

We acknowledge the support of the Government of Canada.

Canada Council   Conseil des arts
for the Arts   du Canada

We gratefully acknowledge for their financial support of our publishing
program the Canada Council for the Arts and the Government of Canada.

story by
Grégoire Laforce

art by
Benjamin Flouw

THE
LOST
DROP

Milky Way
Picture Books

There once was a little drop of water named Flo, who fell from the sky and met the ground for the first time.

She stopped for a moment, looked around, and started to wonder...

"Who am I
and where
should I go?"

But she soon felt a pull in one direction
and began flowing down a slope
into a little stream.

As Flo landed in the stream,
she continued to wonder who
she was and where she should go.

Was this her home?

As she passed by, she asked the trees, the rocks, and the animals if they had seen her before and if they knew where she should go.

They simply nodded and smiled, so Flo continued on her way.

She slid further down the slope and into a lake,
where she brushed up against fishes and sea creatures.

Flo felt the coolness at the bottom of the lake
and the warmth of the sun at the surface.

And still she wondered,
"who am I and where should I go?"

This time, the pull came more quickly,
as Flo was dragged over a ledge,
moving quickly over rocks and crevices.

All of a sudden,
she started falling,
falling, and then...

... stillness.

Things were quieter down here.
The silence was so loud,
it was scary.

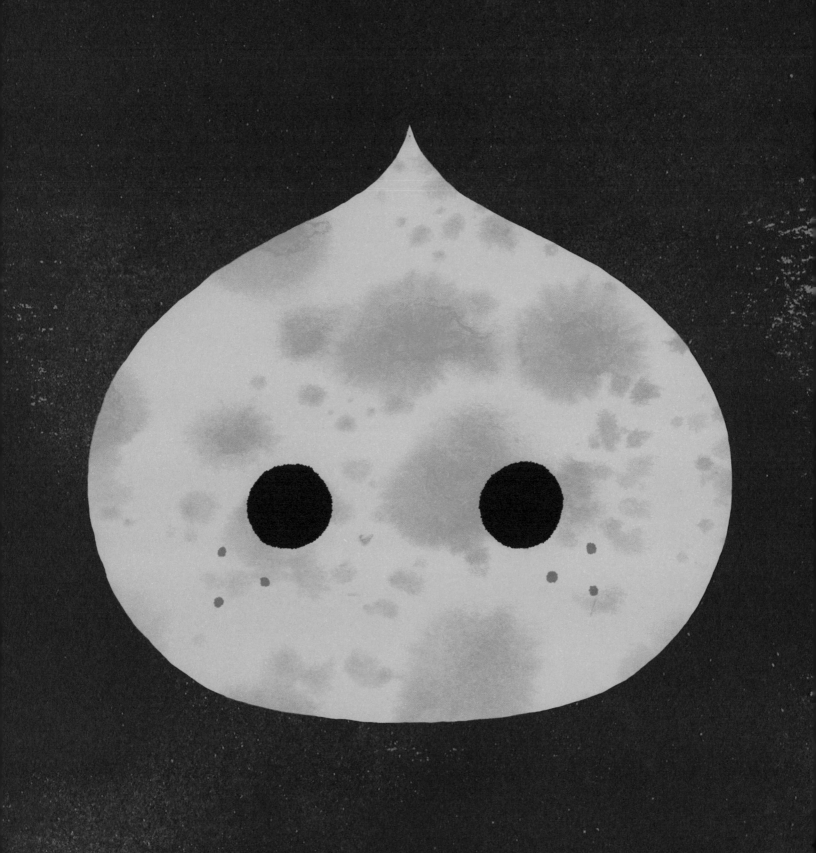

Flo was afraid of these new depths
and wondered for a while
if she had lost her way.

Flo yelled,
"who am I
and where should I go?"

Her question shot out
into the darkness and rippled
back to her. Out and back,
bouncing off the dark walls.

"You are here
and you have nowhere else to go."

Flo recognized the voice

and she laid quietly still.

Suddenly, a huge surge
of light burst forth,

and Flo became
smaller and smaller,
as the warm rays sank
into her being.

Then, something incredible happened.

Flo smiled as she allowed herself
to go with the light.

She almost vanished completely into the air.

But not quite...

Flo helped make the trees dance,

united the breath of all living creatures,

and lifted wings into flight.

After a long and winding journey,

Flo understood that she was finally home.

Did you know that water on Earth has been cycling

since the planet's formation over 4 billion years ago? →

THE WATER CYCLE

CLOUDS
Formed when condensed water vapor in the atmosphere forms a giant, fluffy mass in the sky.

SUBLIMATION
The process by which ice and snow (solid water) change directly into water vapor (a gas) without first becoming liquid water.

PRECIPITATION
The water that falls from the Earth's atmosphere back to the Earth's surface, sometimes in the form of rain, other times in the form of snow.

SNOWMELT

STREAMFLOW
Water that flows through any type of stream (e.g., creeks, rivers, etc.) after returning to the Earth through precipitation.

RUNOFF
Any water that "runs off" of the Earth's surface into a body of water after a precipitation.

TRANSPIRATION
The process by which water vapor is released from plants.

WATERFALL

LAKES
Areas on the Earth's surface where water collects.

INFILTRATION
The process by which water on the surface of the Earth enters into the soil or other porous materials, and reaches the groundwater.

GROUNDWATER RESERVES
Water that is stored underground.

ATMOSPHERE

The Earth's layer of air, through which all forms of water are transported.

CONDENSATION

The process by which water vapor changes from a gas back into a liquid.

SUN

The sun's energy powers the evaporation of water from oceans, lakes, rivers, and other bodies of water, and from the surfaces of plants and other living organisms.

EVAPORATION

The process of water changing from a liquid (like the water we drink!) to a gas.

OCEANS

Earth's largest water reservoirs. They contain over 96% of the Earth's water and, when they evaporate, produce 90% of the water in the Earth's atmosphere.

EVAPOTRANSPIRATION

The combined process of water evaporation from the Earth's surface, such as soil, lakes, rivers, and oceans, and transpiration from plants.

COLLECTION

The process of precipitation collecting in bodies of water such as lakes, oceans, rivers, and streams.

GROUNDWATER FLOW

The movement of water through underground soil, rock, and sediment.